My First Time

Moving House

Kate Petty, Lisa Kopper and Jim Pipe

Aladdin/Watts

London • Sydney

© Aladdin Books Ltd 2007

Designed and produced by

Aladdin Books Ltd
2/3 Fitzroy Mews
London W1T 6DF

First published in 2007

by Franklin Watts
338 Euston Road
London NW1 3BH

Franklin Watts Australia
Level 17/207 Kent Street
Sydney NSW 2000

Franklin Watts is a division of Hachette Children's Books.

ISBN 978 0 7496 7490 8

A catalogue record for
this book is available
from the British Library.

Dewey Classification:
648.9

Printed in China

Illustrator: Lisa Kopper

Photocredits:
All photos from istockphoto.com except 9 — Comstock.

About this book

New experiences can be scary for young children. This series will help them to understand situations they may find themselves in, by explaining in a friendly way what can happen.

This book can be used as a starting point for discussing issues. The questions in some of the boxes ask children about their own experiences.

The stories will also help children to master basic reading skills and learn new vocabulary.

It can help if you read the first sentence to children, and then encourage them to read the rest of the page or story. At the end, try looking through the book again to find where the words in the glossary are used.

Contents

There's a big sign outside the flat where
Sam and Jenny live. It says, "For Sale".

Some people come to see the flat.
They may want to buy it.

4

Sam and Jenny follow Mum as she shows the visitors around.

They like Sam's room — but so does Sam! He doesn't want strangers sleeping there.

Do you live in a house or a flat?

Mum and Dad have found a new house.
They take Sam and Jenny to see it.

There's an upstairs and a downstairs
and a garden.

Outside in the garden Jenny has found a big, friendly dog.

Can they keep him? No, they can't. His owners will take him with them.

Sam has almost forgotten about moving
but this morning a letter arrives.

"We're going to move in three weeks!"
Sam isn't so happy. He likes the flat.

You can carry pets in a special box.

"Will Kitty come with us?" asks Jenny.
"Of course," says Mum, "she's ours."

Sam wonders about the new garden. Surely nobody can take that with them!

Now the whole family is very busy.
Everything has to be packed in boxes.

Mum wraps the delicate things carefully
so they don't break when they're moved.

The flat begins to look very bare
and not a bit like home anymore.

Sam thinks perhaps he won't be sorry
to move to the new house after all.

Today is moving day.
A big van arrives.
The men carry out the furniture.

Sam wonders how they can lift it.
Back and forth, in and out they go.

That looks heavy!

At last everything is neatly packed up.
It's time to follow the van to the
new house. The cat is packed too —
she's safely in her basket. Off they go.

"Here we are. Now we can move in.
Don't let Kitty out, Jenny,"
says Mum.

Sam can't wait to get inside
and explore the empty rooms.

Would you
like to build
a new house?

14

The moving men start unloading.
In and out of the house they go again and again.

Sam rushes out to meet the neighbours.
Jenny will have to meet them tomorrow.

At last the van is empty.
The men say goodbye.

The kitchen things are
still packed so Dad
gets a take-away.

Jenny wonders where the cat is.
She's safe and sound, but rather angry.

She'd like some food too!

Sam goes upstairs to his very own room.
They've never had an "upstairs" before.

Jenny's fast asleep already.
Dad takes her up to bed.

She's sleeping alone tonight so Dad leaves the door open.

Dad has promised to paint Sam's room. Sam wonders what colour to choose.

What colour paint would you choose?

19

Now Sam has gone to sleep too.
Mum and Dad carry on working.

One by one the boxes are unpacked
and the house begins to look like home.

Kitty sniffs and prowls around.

But when Mum and Dad sit down,
Kitty settles between them on the sofa.
She has a garden to explore tomorrow.

"For Sale"
sign

packing

moving van

keys

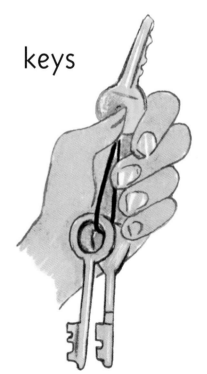

furniture

boxes

upstairs

downstairs

23

Index

Find out more

Find out more about moving house at:

http://www.netdoctor.co.uk/health_advice/facts/movinghouse.htm
http://www.helpiammoving.com/moving_house/moving_with_children.php
http://www.themovechannel.com/guides/Moving/Coping/
http://www.bishopsmove.net/residential/guidepets.html